Best Prank Ever

Ready, Freddy!

#1: Tooth Trouble
#2: The King of Show-and-Tell
#3: Homework Hassles
#4: Don't Sit on My Lunch!
#5: Talent Show Scaredy-Pants
#6: Help! A Vampire's Coming!
#7: Yikes! Bikes!
#8: Halloween Fraidy-Cat
#9: Shark Tooth Tale
#10: Super-Secret Valentine
#11: The Pumpkin Elf Mystery
#12: Stop That Hamster!
#13: The One Hundredth Day of School!
#14: Camping Catastrophe!
#15: Thanksgiving Turkey Trouble
#16: Ready, Set, Snow!
#17: Firehouse Fun!
#18: The Perfect Present
#19: The Penguin Problem
#20: Apple Orchard Race
#21: Going Batty
#22: Science Fair Flop
#23: A Very Crazy Christmas
#24: Shark Attack!
#25: Save the Earth!
#26: The Giant Swing
#27: The Reading Race

2nd Grade

#1: Second Grade Rules!
#2: Snow Day Dare
#3: Secret Santa Surprise
#4: Best Prank Ever

Best Prank Ever

by ABBY KLEIN

illustrated by
JOHN McKINLEY

Scholastic Inc.

To Jenson,
Super baby and future prankster!
Love,
A.K.

ISBN 978-0-545-86358-2

10 9 8 7 6 5   17 18 19 20

Printed in the U.S.A   40

First printing 2016

CHAPTERS

1. March 31 9

2. Ideas, Anyone? 20

3. Suzie the Snoop 29

4. Kasey and Kelly's Pranks 40

5. The Plan 49

6. The Night Before 59

7. April Fools' Day: Part 1 68

8. April Fools' Day: Part 2 78

Freddy's Fun Pages 89

I have a problem.

A really, really big problem.

Tomorrow is April Fools' Day, and I
don't know any good tricks to play on
my friends and family.

Let me tell you about it.

CHAPTER 1

March 31

"Tomorrow is a new month," said my teacher, Miss Clark. "Does anybody know what month starts tomorrow?"

"I do! I do!" Chloe squealed, waving her mint-green fingernails in the air. "Tomorrow is April first."

"That's correct," said Miss Clark, "and it's a special day."

"I know it is," Chloe continued. "It's the day

I get a new manicure and change the color of my nail polish."

"Is she kidding?" Josh whispered.

"I wish," Jessie whispered back. "Unfortunately, she's not. She's for real."

"On the first day of every month," Chloe was telling Miss Clark, "I go to the nail salon and get my nails painted a different color."

"Unbelievable," Josh mumbled, shaking his head.

"For the month of March, I painted my nails green for Saint Patrick's Day," Chloe said. "I'm not sure yet what color I'll paint my nails for April. Easter is in April, so I'll probably paint them a pretty pastel color. Maybe lavender or —"

"No one cares!" Max interrupted loudly.

Chloe stopped talking about her nails and turned to Max. "What did you say?"

"I said, 'No one cares!'" Max barked.

"Says who?" Chloe demanded.

"Says everyone in this room," said Max.

"That's not true," said Chloe.

"Yes, it is," said Max. "Ask anyone."

"Okay, I will." Chloe turned to Josh and smiled sweetly. "Josh, you care what color I paint my nails, right?"

I poked Josh in the side. "Now you're in trouble," I whispered.

Josh stammered, "I, uh — I, uh —"

Just then Miss Clark interrupted him. "Chloe, your nails are very pretty, but that is not what I was talking about when I said that tomorrow is a special day."

"Whew, that was a close one," I whispered to Josh. "Nice save by Miss Clark."

Josh nodded, looking relieved.

"I know why tomorrow is special," said Jessie.

"Great!" said Miss Clark. "Tell the class."

"Tomorrow is April Fools' Day."

Max jumped out of his seat and pumped his fist in the air. "I love April Fools' Day! It's the best day ever."

"Have you ever played any April Fools' tricks on anyone?" asked Miss Clark.

"It doesn't have to be April Fools' for him to play tricks on people," I whispered to Josh. "He's the biggest bully in the whole second grade. He does mean things to kids all the time."

"Oh yeah," said Max, snickering. "I've done some great tricks on April Fools' Day."

"Like what?" asked Miss Clark.

"Last year I put some salt in Freddy's water bottle when he wasn't looking. You should have seen his face when he took a sip of water! Ha, ha, ha, ha!"

"Did he really do that to you?" Josh asked.

"Yep." I nodded. "He thought it was hilarious."

"I remember that," said Chloe. "That wasn't very funny."

"Yes, it was," said Max. "It was *really* funny!"

"Well, I didn't think so," said Chloe. "You're just a big meanie."

"You'd better be careful, or I just might play a trick on you this year," said Max.

"Oh no you wouldn't," said Chloe.

"Oh yes I would."

"No you wouldn't."

"Yes I would," Max said, grinning. "I'm thinking of some good ones right now."

"Miss Clark! Miss Clark!" Chloe whined. "Max is going to play a trick on me."

"He's just saying that to annoy you," said Miss Clark. "Ignore him."

"Have you ever played tricks on anyone, Miss Clark?" Jessie asked.

"Yes, I have, Jessie," said Miss Clark.

"Wow! She is the coolest teacher ever," Josh said.

"I like April Fools' Day pranks," Miss Clark said, "but I prefer the kind that are funny *and* harmless."

"What's one of your favorite tricks?" Jessie asked.

Miss Clark smiled. "I remember, one time when I was a kid, I put a blown-up balloon in the toilet and shut the lid. When my sister went to go to the bathroom, she opened the lid, and surprise . . . a balloon floated up into her face. She screamed, and I laughed hysterically. It was so funny!"

"That's a good one," Jessie said.

"I should try that on my sister," I said.

"Oh, I have another good one," Max said. "You take the salt out of your saltshaker and replace it with sugar. Then when your mom goes to put salt on her eggs in the morning, she's actually putting sugar on them! Her eggs taste really sweet and disgusting!" Max was rolling with laughter.

"That's an old one," Josh said. "I've heard that before. That's not very original."

Max stopped laughing and glared at Josh.

"Uh-oh," I said. "He's giving you the evil eye."

"Whatever," said Josh. "He can give me the evil eye all he wants. He doesn't scare me. You've got to stop being so afraid of him, Freddy."

"I thought it would be fun to celebrate April Fools' Day tomorrow by making it Backwards Day," said Miss Clark.

"Backwards Day? What's that?" asked Jessie.

"We wear our clothes backwards," said Miss Clark.

"What do you mean?" Chloe asked.

"You just put everything on backwards," Jessie said.

"That's right," said Miss Clark. "You put your shirt, pants, and even your underwear on the wrong way. You'll have to keep your shoes on straight, though, or you won't be able to walk!"

"I don't think I can do that," said Chloe, "because I have to wear a dress."

"Sure you can," Miss Clark told her. "You turn the dress around and wear the zipper in the front."

Chloe frowned. "That doesn't sound very fun."

"Just try it," said Miss Clark. "You'll see. It will be lots of fun."

"With your undies on backwards, it will be harder to give you a wedgie," Max whispered to me. "But I'll come up with some other good tricks. Better watch out."

I gulped.

"No, *you'd* better watch out," said Josh. "We'll have some good tricks of our own. Right, Freddy?"

I nodded and smiled weakly. "Right."

CHAPTER 2

Ideas, Anyone?

That afternoon on the bus ride home Josh said, "So, Freddy, we have to come up with something really good for tomorrow."

"What are you guys talking about?" said my other best friend, Robbie.

"Tomorrow is April Fools' Day," said Josh.

"Oh yeah, I almost forgot," said Robbie. "Good thing you guys reminded me."

"We have to come up with a good trick to play on Max," said Josh.

"On Max?" Robbie said a bit too loudly.

"Hey, you wimps," Max said, standing up in his seat. "Did one of you just call my name?"

"Uh-oh," I whispered.

"No," said Josh. "Maybe you should have your hearing checked."

"Good one," Robbie whispered.

"No standing up in the bus!" the bus driver yelled over his shoulder. "Sit down, Max."

Max flopped back down in his seat.

"Are you really going to play a trick on Max?" Robbie asked.

"Yeah, why not?" asked Josh.

"Because he's the biggest bully in the whole second grade," said Robbie. "Everyone is afraid of him."

"Well, I'm not," said Josh. "He's always playing tricks on kids. Someone should play a trick on him. Let's see how he likes it."

Robbie turned to me. "You're going to do this, too, Freddy?"

"Of course he is!" said Josh.

I nodded slowly.

"He played a trick on Freddy last year, so why shouldn't Freddy play a trick on him this year?"

"He did?" said Robbie.

"Yeah, remember? He put salt in my water bottle."

"Oh yeah," Robbie said chuckling. "How could I forget? You made the funniest face when you took that first sip!"

I scrunched up my nose.

"And then you spit it out all over your desk," said Robbie.

"You did?" said Josh. "I wish I had been there to see that!"

"It was disgusting," I said. "Have you ever tasted salt water?"

"Lots of times," said Josh.

"You have?" said Robbie.

"When I went surfing in California, I used to swallow a lot of salt water by accident. It doesn't taste good."

"I've never been to the beach," said Robbie. "I've only gone swimming in pools, and pool water is pretty disgusting, too!"

"I think I swallowed, like, half the pool the last time I went swimming," I said, laughing.

"This summer I'm going to have to teach you to be a better swimmer," said Josh.

"Cool," I said.

"So, do you guys know what trick you're going to play on Max?" asked Robbie.

"Nope," said Josh. "Got any good ideas?"

"Hmmm . . . let's see," said Robbie. "You could do something with fake bugs."

"Like what?" I said.

"Like sneak one into his sandwich at lunchtime, so when he goes to take a bite, he gets a bug in his mouth."

I laughed. "That could be good," I said.

"Nah," said Josh. "We need something better."

"But remember we played that bug trick on Chloe?" I said. "We put that fake spider in her cubby, and she freaked out."

"But that's Chloe," said Josh. "She's afraid of everything."

"Good point," said Robbie.

"Max is not afraid of bugs," Josh continued. "He's not going to freak out because we put a plastic bug in his sandwich."

"I guess you're right." I sighed.

"Oh, I just thought of a good one," said Josh.

"What?" I said.

"Have you ever dropped a can of soda on the ground by accident right before you were going to open it?"

"I did once," said Robbie.

"And what happened when you went to open it?" said Josh.

"The whole thing exploded in my face," Robbie said, laughing.

"Really?" I said.

"Really. My hair was dripping with soda, and my shirt was soaked!"

"Same thing happened to me," said Josh.

"I wonder why that happens," I said.

"It's because of the carbon dioxide," Robbie said.

"The what?" said Josh.

"The carbon dioxide. It's what makes soda bubbly. Carbon dioxide is a gas that usually sits at the top of the can, but if you shake the can, the carbon dioxide gets mixed around with the liquid soda below it. Because the gas is not sitting by itself at the top of the can anymore, when you open it, the bubbles come rushing out from all different parts of the container, making the liquid soda explode in your face!"

"Thank you, Einstein," I said.

"What are you?" said Josh. "Some kind of science genius?"

"Yes, he is," I said. "He is like a walking encyclopedia of science."

"Wow! I'm impressed," said Josh.

"I just really like science," Robbie said, smiling.

"There's only one problem with that prank," I said.

"What?" said Josh.

"We're not allowed to have soda at school."

"Shoot," said Josh. "I would have loved to see soda explode in Max Sellars's face."

"That would have been awesome," I said, "but we'll have to think of something else."

"I don't really have any more ideas," Josh said.

"Me either," said Robbie.

"And we don't have a lot of time," said Josh. "April Fools' is tomorrow!"

"I just got a great idea!" I said suddenly.

"Awesome! What is it?" asked Josh.

"I have twin cousins named Kasey and Kelly. People call them Double Trouble because they are always getting into trouble. I know they'll have some really good April Fools' Day tricks. I'll call them as soon as I get home and see what ideas they have. Then why don't you come over, and we can make a plan."

"I'll just drop off my backpack at home and come over to your house," said Josh.

"Me, too," said Robbie.

"Great! See you guys in about half an hour," I said as the bus pulled up in front of my house.

"You'd better be careful tomorrow," Max said as I passed by his seat, getting off the bus. "You never know what might happen."

No, you'd *better be careful,* I thought to myself, and smiled.

CHAPTER 3

Suzie the Snoop

"Mom, I'm home!" I yelled as I kicked the front door closed behind me and dropped my backpack on the floor.

"Freddy, how many times have I told you to close the door with your hands, not your feet?"

"Sorry, Mom. I just forget."

"Using your foot leaves dirty shoe prints on the door. Now I have to go get something to clean that up."

My mom is such a neat freak. She is always cleaning something. She walked into the laundry room to get a sponge and some cleaner. I followed her in there. "Hey, Mom, can I have Kelly and Kasey's phone number?"

She grabbed what she needed and headed back to the front door. I went with her.

"Your cousins? Why do you want their phone number?"

"Because, um . . . because . . . I need their advice for a project at school."

"Well, that's nice," my mom said, scrubbing my shoe print off the door. Just then the door flung open, and my mom went flying backwards.

"Mom! Are you okay?" my sister, Suzie, asked.

"Yes, honey, I'm fine. You just took me by surprise."

"I'm so sorry. I had no idea you were behind the door. What were you doing there, anyway?"

"Trying to clean some muddy shoe prints left by your brother."

"So, Mom, can I have their number?" I asked again.

"Whose number?" said Suzie.

"Kasey and Kelly's number."

"Why do you want their phone number?"

"None of your beeswax," I said.

"Mom, Freddy must be up to something naughty if he won't tell me why he wants their number."

I glared at Suzie.

"He's not up to anything naughty," my mom said. "He just wants their phone number so he can get their help with a project for school."

"Really?" said Suzie, staring right at me. "What kind of project?"

"It's a secret," I said. "If I told you, it would ruin the surprise."

"This whole thing sounds really fishy to me," said Suzie. "Doesn't it, Mom?"

"Oh, Suzie, leave your brother alone. I think it's nice that he wants to talk to his cousins."

"Thanks, Mom," I said.

My mom finished wiping the door and went to put the cleaning supplies away.

"I know you're up to something," Suzie said. "Don't think I won't find out."

"Whatever," I said, and walked into the kitchen.

My mom came in and picked up the phone.

"Should I dial your cousins' number for you, Freddy?"

"Uh, actually, could you just write it down on a piece of paper for me? I want to call them myself."

"Sure, honey," my mom said.

She wrote the number down and handed it to me along with the phone. I started to head upstairs.

"Where are you going?" Suzie called after me.

"To my room. Is that okay with you?"

"See, Mom," said Suzie. "Freddy must be up to something if he's calling them from his room."

"He just wants some privacy," said my mom. "He said it was a surprise, so he doesn't want us to hear the conversation."

As I got to the top of the stairs, I could hear footsteps behind me. I turned around to see Suzie following me.

"What are you doing?" I asked.

"Just going up to my room, if that's okay with you," she said. "I need to get something."

"I think you're following me."

"Really?"

"Really. You're being a snoop. You always have to know everyone else's business."

"That's not true," Suzie said.

"Yes, it is. Why don't you mind your own business for once?" I said as I went into my room and slammed the door.

"You are so annoying!" Suzie yelled through my door. "I was just going to my own room!"

I waited a few seconds, and then I heard Suzie slam her bedroom door shut.

She thinks I'm so stupid that I don't know her little tricks, I thought to myself. *She shut her door so I would think she went into her room. I bet she is still standing right out in the hallway with her ear pressed up against my door, trying to hear my phone call.*

I waited a few more seconds, and then I tiptoed over to my door and yanked it open. Suzie toppled onto my bedroom floor.

"Ha! I knew it!" I said. "I knew you didn't really go into your own room. You wanted me to think you did, but you really didn't. I'm going to call you Suzie the Snoop."

Suzie stood up and glared at me. "There is a reason people call Kasey and Kelly Double Trouble. They're always doing crazy things. If you're calling them, it's because you're planning on doing something naughty."

"Like I said. I need their help for something at school. Now, get out of my room and leave me alone, or I'll tell Mom."

Suzie didn't budge.

"Mom!" I shouted. "Mom!"

Suzie put her hand over my mouth. "Shhh! You'll get me in trouble."

"That's the point," I said.

"Fine. I'll leave you alone," she said as she

turned to walk out of my room. "But I know you're up to something, and I'm going to find out what."

I pointed to my door. "Get out now!"

"I'm going, I'm going," Suzie said as she left.

I stood in my doorway and watched her disappear downstairs.

"I knew she didn't really need anything from her room," I muttered to myself.

I went back into my room and closed the door. I sat down on my bed and dialed my cousins' number.

"Hello?"

"Hello," I said. "Is this Kasey or Kelly?" I can never tell them apart. They sound exactly the same.

"This is Kelly. Who's this?"

"It's Freddy."

"Freddy? Really? It's so cool you called. Let me get Kasey to pick up the other phone so we can all talk at the same time."

Kasey picked up the phone. "Freddy! We haven't seen you in so long. What's up?"

"I need your help with something."

"Sure!" they both said. "What is it?"

"April Fools' Day," I said.

They laughed. "Good thing you called, because we are April Fools' Day experts!"

CHAPTER 4

Kasey and Kelly's Pranks

"I figured you guys knew some really good April Fools' Day tricks," I said to Kasey and Kelly.

"We sure do!" said Kelly.

"April Fools' Day is one of our favorite holidays!" said Kasey.

"Here's a good one," said Kelly. "You tie a rubber band around the handle of the sprayer hose on your kitchen sink. Then when your mom turns on the water in the morning, she gets sprayed in the face."

"Ha, ha, ha! That's so funny. Did you guys ever do that to your mom?" I asked.

"We did it last year," said Kasey. "It was great! You should have seen her. She was soaking wet."

"She looked like she just got out of the shower," said Kelly, laughing.

"I bet she was really angry."

"She didn't get too mad. It's only water. She just made us clean it up," said Kasey.

"I might have to try that one on my mom this year," I said.

"You should!" said Kelly. "It's hilarious! If you do, take a picture with your mom's phone and send it to us. I'd love to see Aunt Debbie soaking wet. I can picture it right now!"

"You just have to put the rubber band on the sprayer late at night when everyone has gone to sleep. You don't want anyone to see you doing it. And remember to turn the sprayer so it's facing up. That way as soon as your mom turns on the water, she'll get blasted in the face."

"I definitely think I'm going to try that, but actually, I was looking for tricks to play on other kids."

"Oh, I get it," said Kelly. "You want to play a trick on Suzie."

"I have a great one for Suzie," said Kasey.

"Really?"

"Yeah. You want to hear it?"

"Sure," I said. I wasn't planning on playing a trick on Suzie, but if it was a good one, then maybe I would. After all, she'd been really annoying me lately, and I was tired of her snooping.

"For this prank you need some of those washable markers. Do you have those?"

"I think so," I said.

"Make *sure* they're washable," said Kasey. "You definitely don't want to use permanent ones."

"Yeah, if you use permanent ones, you'll get in a lot of trouble," said Kelly. "Trust me on this one."

42

"Okay, so what's the trick?" I asked.

"You have to do this one late at night, too," said Kasey. "You sneak into Suzie's room when she's asleep . . ."

"I like it so far," I said. "Keep talking."

"You sneak in when she's asleep and draw something funny on her face."

"Last year we snuck into Kenny's room and drew a mustache on his face."

"You did? That must have been hilarious!" I said.

"It was. It really was," said Kelly, chuckling. "Kasey and I laughed about it for days."

"We took a picture of little Kenny with his mustache, and even now when we need a good laugh, we take out that picture."

"I'll definitely have to do that to Suzie this year. I just have to figure out what to draw."

"Oh! I have the best idea," said Kasey.

"What?"

"Why don't you draw little red marks all

over her face? When she goes into the bathroom in the morning and looks in the mirror, she'll think she has chicken pox!"

"Ha, ha, ha! That's awesome!" I said. "She will totally freak out!"

"Yes, she will," said Kelly. "Suzie will definitely freak out!"

"These are really great ideas," I said, "and I'm probably going to use both of them, but I still need some ideas of tricks I can play on kids at school."

"Who are you going to play a trick on?" asked Kasey.

"Max Sellars."

"Is that the Max you're always talking about?" asked Kelly.

"Yep."

"The one who you say is the biggest bully in the whole second grade?"

"Yes, that's the one."

"Ooh, then we have to help you come up with something really good," said Kasey.

"Yeah. Really, really good," Kelly said, snickering.

Just then there was a knock at my door.

"Hang on a second, guys," I whispered to Kasey and Kelly. "Someone just knocked on my door."

I put the phone down and walked over to the door. "Who is it?" I yelled.

"It's me," Suzie said.

"I thought I told you to stop snooping."

"I'm not snooping," Suzie said. "Mom asked me to bring you a snack."

"Nice try," I said, still not opening the door. "I know you don't have a snack for me. Mom never lets us eat anything in our rooms. You're still just trying to spy on me. Go away!"

"UGH!" Suzie groaned, and stomped away.

I picked up the phone again. "Sorry about that. Suzie was snooping around again. She wants to know why I'm calling you."

"You didn't tell her, did you?" asked Kasey.

"Of course not!" I said. "That would ruin everything!"

"So, Kasey and I have a great idea for Max," said Kelly.

"Are you ready, Freddy?" asked Kasey.

"Tell me! Tell me!"

"Does he like cookies?"

"Oh, he's like a cookie monster," I said. "He *loves* cookies!"

"Great!" said Kelly. "Then this will be perfect. Take some Oreo cookies, pull them apart, and carefully scrape out the white cream filling in the center. Then replace the filling with white toothpaste and put the cookies back together."

"Then bring the cookies to school," said Kasey, "and tell Max you brought him a special snack."

"If he loves cookies as much as you say he does, then he'll practically grab the cookies right out of your hands!" said Kelly.

"Awesome! That is so awesome!" I said. "I can't wait to see his face when he bites into that cookie."

"We have to go now," said Kasey and Kelly. "Call us tomorrow and let us know how everything goes."

"Don't worry. I will," I said. "Thanks so much for the great ideas. You guys are the best!"

"It was great talking to you, Freddy! Happy April Fools' Day!"

"Bye, cuz."

"Bye!" I hung up the phone and smiled. *This is going to be the best April Fools' Day ever!* I thought to myself.

CHAPTER 5

The Plan

There was another knock on my bedroom door, and then it started to open. I ran over to shove it closed. "Hey, I thought I told you to leave me alone!" I shouted.

"Freddy, it's just us," said Robbie and Josh through the door.

"Oh, come in, guys," I said, opening the door. "I thought you were Suzie. She keeps snooping around my room, trying to figure out what I'm up to."

"Big sisters can be so annoying sometimes," Robbie said. "Kimberly does the same thing to me."

"So did you talk to your cousins?" asked Josh.

"I just got off the phone with them."

"Did they have any good ideas?" asked Robbie.

"They had a bunch of good ideas. They even had some good ideas of tricks I can play on my mom and Suzie."

"Cool," said Josh. "They sound like a lot of fun!"

"They are," I said. "Last time when they came to visit for Christmas, it turned out to be one crazy Christmas!"

"So what was their idea for Max?"

"You know how much he loves cookies, right?" I said.

"Oh, he's like a cookie monster," said Josh.

"That's exactly what I said!"

"He always has cookies for a snack, like a gazillion of them," said Josh.

"And what is his favorite kind?"

"Oh, that's easy," said Josh. "Oreos, of course."

"So Kasey and Kelly said we should take the cream filling out of an Oreo, replace it with white toothpaste, and then put the cookie back together. Then we just switch one of his Oreos for our 'special' one."

"Ha, ha, ha! That is awesome!" said Josh. "I love that idea."

"That is a really great idea," said Robbie.

"So now we have to make our super-secret April Fools' Day plan," I said.

"That's easy," said Josh. "Do you have Oreos in your house, Freddy?"

"Of course I do! They're one of my favorite cookies. I love breaking them apart, licking out the cream in the middle, and then dunking the chocolate cookie part into my milk."

"Hey, I do the exact same thing!" said Josh, smiling.

"So does Robbie," I said.

"You do?" said Josh.

"Yep," said Robbie, nodding his head. "I do!"

"No wonder we're all such good friends," I said.

"So we just have to go downstairs, get some Oreos, bring one up to your room, scrape out the middle, and put in the toothpaste," said Josh. "Easy peasy."

"Not as easy as you think," said Robbie.

"Why not?" asked Josh.

"Because Freddy's mom is a neat freak. He's not allowed to have any food in his room."

"Really? I have snacks in my room all the time," said Josh.

"I wish," I said. "We're only allowed to eat in the kitchen."

"So we'll have to sneak the Oreo out of the kitchen somehow."

"How are we going to do that?" I asked.

"We can go down there, ask your mom for some Oreos as a snack, and then when she's not looking, you hide some in your pocket."

"That should work," said Robbie.

"What do you think, Freddy?" said Josh.

"Let's go!" I said.

We raced downstairs into the kitchen. "Hello, boys," said my mom. "What's up?"

"I just realized that I never had a snack when I came home," I said. "Can we have something now?"

"Sure! What about some cheese and crackers?" asked my mom.

"I was thinking more like Oreos and milk."

"Okay," said my mom, "but only two cookies each. I don't want you to spoil your dinner."

"I'll get the cookies, Mom, while you get the milk."

"Thanks, Freddy."

"No problem, Mom."

I grabbed the bag of cookies and brought them to the table. While my mom was busy pouring glasses of milk for each of us, I stuffed an Oreo in my pocket and gave Robbie and Josh a thumbs-up.

"Here you go, boys," said my mom, handing us the milk. "Now remember, only two cookies each."

"Sure thing, Mrs. Thresher," said Josh.

"Only two," Robbie said, showing my mom a cookie in each hand.

After we finished licking and dunking, we went back upstairs to my room and shut the door.

I took the cookie out of my pocket.

"Good. It didn't get crushed," said Robbie.

"First we have to get the filling out," said Josh. "Do you have a knife?"

"We don't need a knife," I said, smiling. I carefully opened the Oreo and licked out the cream filling.

"Ewww!" said Robbie, "now it has your germs."

"Even better!" Josh said, laughing.

"Now go get the toothpaste," said Josh.

I had to sneak into my parents' bathroom because they had the plain white toothpaste.

My toothpaste had sparkles in it, and that wouldn't work.

I was grabbing the toothpaste off the counter when Suzie walked up behind me and startled me. "AAAAHHH!" I screamed.

"What are you doing in here?" she asked.

"What are *you* doing in here?"

"Why do you need Mom and Dad's toothpaste?"

"None of your business."

"Maybe I should tell Mom that you're in here."

"You wouldn't do that."

"Oh really?" Suzie said smiling. "Watch me." She started to yell for my mom, but I covered her mouth.

"SHHHH!"

"What's it worth to you?" Suzie said.

"You can have my dessert tonight," I said.

"Tonight?" said Suzie. "How about for the next three nights?"

"Three nights? You're crazy!"

"It's three nights or nothing," said Suzie, holding up her pinky for a pinky swear.

I really needed that toothpaste. "Fine," I said locking pinkies with her. "Three nights."

I pushed past Suzie and rushed back to my room.

"What took you so long?" asked Josh.

"Don't ask," I said. "But I got the toothpaste."

"Great! Now we just have to spread it around to look like cream filling."

I spread the toothpaste around with my finger and then put the top of the cookie back on. "Perfect!" I said.

"It looks just like a real Oreo," said Josh.

"I can't wait until tomorrow," I said.

"I'm just sorry I won't be there to see Max's face when he takes a bite of that cookie," said Robbie.

"It's going to be great!" said Josh. "The best prank ever!"

CHAPTER 6

The Night Before

"Good night, Freddy."

"Good night, Dad."

"Good night, Freddy."

"Good night, Mom."

My mom felt my forehead. "Are you feeling all right?" she asked.

"Yeah, I'm fine. Why?"

"Well, you didn't eat your dessert tonight, and dessert is your favorite thing in the whole world. Instead, you gave your dessert to Suzie."

"I . . . uh . . . I . . . uh . . . just didn't feel like ice cream."

"Wait a minute. You must be sick if you don't feel like ice cream," said my dad, laughing. "You would eat ice cream for breakfast, lunch, and dinner if we let you!"

"I was just too full from that awesome lasagna Mom made."

"Well, all right," said my dad.

"We'll see how you're feeling in the morning," said my mom.

"I'll be fine."

"Sleep well. See you in the morning," said my mom.

"Yep. See you in the morning."

"Get a good night's sleep," said my dad.

"Oh, I will. Good night."

Little did they know I was going to be up half the night!

I waited until my parents' footsteps disappeared down the hall, and then I pulled my covers over my head and turned on my shark-head flashlight. I had to do something to keep myself awake. I had work to do once everyone went to sleep.

I sorted through my baseball cards for a while.

I read some of my favorite books.

I drew some pictures.

When the house seemed silent, I tiptoed over to my bedroom door and slowly opened it. I peeked out into the hallway. It looked like the coast was clear.

I pushed up my pajama sleeve to make sure that the rubber band I had put around my wrist was still there. It was.

Grabbing my flashlight, I crept out into the hall. I would have to wait to turn my flashlight on until I was downstairs or else the light might wake up my parents.

I walked very slowly to the top of the stairs and felt along the wall for the railing. I held on tight and made my way down, making sure to skip the step that creaks.

I tiptoed into the kitchen and turned on my flashlight, so I could see my way to the sink. Once I got there, I put the flashlight down on the counter and aimed it at the sprayer, so I could see what I was doing.

"This is going to be so funny!" I said to myself. "Mom is going to be so surprised!"

I took the rubber band off my wrist and wrapped it once around the button on the sprayer. Then I put the sprayer back in place.

I'd better wrap the rubber band around a few more times, I thought. *I want to make sure it's on there good and tight.*

I grabbed the sprayer and wrapped the rubber band around a few more times. "There. That should work."

I put the sprayer back. *Wait,* I thought. *Kasey told me to make sure I did something with the sprayer. What was it? Oh yeah, she said to put the sprayer back facing up.*

I turned the sprayer so the water would shoot right into my mom's face, as soon as she turned on the water.

As long as I was down in the kitchen, I decided to have a little midnight snack. I had missed out on dessert since I had to give mine to Suzie because of our deal, so I would have some ice cream now. I didn't want to put it in a bowl because my mom would see the dirty dish in the sink in the morning, so I grabbed a spoon and ate it right out of the container. It was delicious! My dad was right. I could eat this stuff for breakfast, lunch, and dinner.

I licked off my spoon and put it back in the silverware drawer. I grabbed my flashlight and tiptoed back to the stairs. I turned off my light

and quietly went back upstairs, making sure once again to skip the creaky step.

"Now for secret mission number two," I whispered to myself.

I first went back into my room to get the red washable marker I had hidden in my underwear drawer. I had to make sure I opened the drawer really slowly, so it wouldn't make a sound.

I felt around with my hands in the dark and found the marker underneath a pile of underwear. I pulled it out and crept over to my door and back out into the hallway. The house was still silent.

I went into Suzie's room. This mission would be a little trickier. I couldn't use the flashlight because the light would wake up Suzie for sure, and I would be in so much trouble if she woke up while I was writing on her face!

I got down on my hands and knees and crawled over to her bed. Suzie was sleeping on her side.

I stood up quietly and leaned over the bed. I was about to start drawing on her face when Suzie snorted and rolled over. I thought she was going to wake up, so I ducked underneath her bed and held my breath.

I waited under the bed for a minute, but she didn't wake up. She just started snoring really loudly. I had to cover my mouth so I wouldn't laugh out loud!

I crawled out from underneath the bed. *It's now or never,* I thought to myself.

I bent down and started making red dots all over her face as quickly as I could. Luckily, Suzie sleeps with a night-light, so I could kind of see what I was doing.

As soon as I finished the last dot, I crawled back out of her room, dashed into my room, and threw the pen back into my underwear drawer. Then I jumped into bed.

Phew! Mission accomplished, I thought to myself. *Tomorrow is going to be so great! I don't*

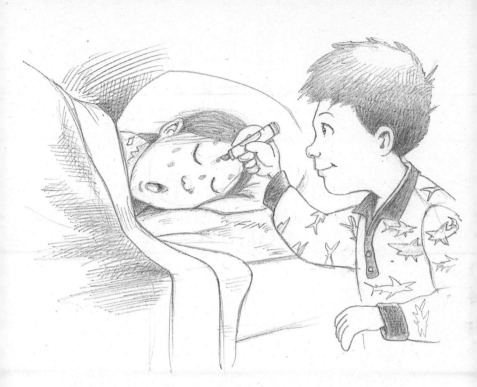

even need an alarm clock. I will wake up to the screams of my mom and sister.

I pulled up my covers and smiled to myself. *But the best part will be watching Max Sellars, the biggest bully in the whole second grade, eat an Oreo full of toothpaste!*

CHAPTER 7

April Fools' Day: Part 1

"AAAAAAHHHHH!!"

Suzie's scream woke me up at exactly 6:30 A.M. I smiled to myself.

My parents came running out of their bedroom. "Suzie, are you okay? What's wrong?"

"Look at my face!" she screamed. "I have red marks all over my face!"

I ran into the bathroom to join them. "What's going on?" I asked. "What's all the screaming about?"

"Suzie has red marks all over her face," said my dad.

"You do?" I said, pretending not to know what they were all taking about.

"Yes! See for yourself," Suzie said, turning to look at me.

"Yikes!" I said. "That looks pretty bad."

"Thanks a lot," said Suzie.

"What do you think it is, Mom?" I asked.

"I'm not sure."

"Do you think it could be chicken pox?" I said.

"What did you just say?" Suzie shouted. "Chicken pox?"

"Yeah. I've never had them, but it looks like chicken pox to me."

"No! No! It can't be chicken pox! I have my big dance recital coming up next week," said Suzie.

"Calm down, Suzie," said my mom.

"Calm down? Calm down? I have chicken pox, and you want me to calm down?"

I had to turn around and hide my face because I was about to burst out laughing. This April Fools' Day prank was turning out even better than I expected.

"Maybe it's not chicken pox," said my dad. "After all, Freddy isn't a doctor."

"That's true," said my mom. "Maybe it's just a rash from something you ate last night."

"I didn't eat anything different last night," said Suzie.

"Maybe you got a rash because you ate too much ice cream," I said. "Remember, you had two helpings, yours and mine."

Suzie glared at me. "I didn't get a rash from eating too much ice cream."

"Why don't you try washing your face?" I suggested.

"That's a stupid suggestion," said Suzie. "Rashes don't wash off."

"Well, at least rinse your face with a cold

washcloth," said my mom. "That might stop the itching."

"Is it itchy?" asked my dad.

"Yes!" Suzie said, scratching her face.

This was hilarious! Suzie was scratching at red dots made by a marker!

"Here's a washcloth, honey," said my mom. "Just run it under cold water and rub it on your face."

Suzie rinsed the washcloth in the sink and started to wipe down her face.

"Make sure you rub it over your whole face," my mom said.

Suzie gently wiped her face for a few seconds while my parents stared at her.

"Wait a minute," said my mom. "Why is the washcloth turning red?"

"What?" said Suzie.

My mom grabbed the washcloth from her. "Look! The washcloth is turning red."

"That's weird," said my dad.

"Suzie, turn toward me," said my mom. "I want to see something."

My mom took the washcloth and rubbed it on Suzie's face a little bit harder. "The marks are coming off!"

"What do you mean, the marks are coming off?" asked my dad.

"I mean that they are washing right off!" said my mom. "This isn't a rash. This looks like red washable marker."

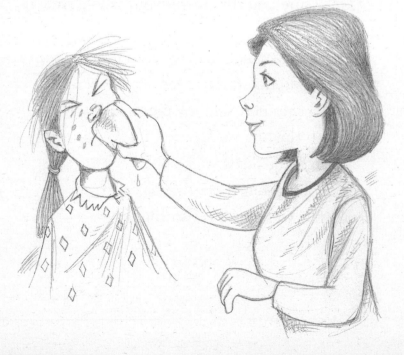

Just then everyone turned to look at me.

I smiled a big, wide smile. "April Fools'!" I yelled. "Gotcha!" Then I started laughing hysterically.

"It is *so* not funny!" Suzie yelled. "Why you little —"

"Oh, come on, Suzie," said my dad. "Where's your sense of humor? I think that was a pretty good trick your brother played on you, and it was perfectly harmless. Look! It washed right off."

"Well, it's getting late. I need to go downstairs and start breakfast," said my mom. "You two, get dressed and come down to eat."

My mom disappeared down the stairs, and I went back into my bedroom. I waited about one minute, and then I heard it — the second scream.

"AAAAAAHHHHH!"

Once again, I smiled to myself.

My mom came stomping up the stairs with her hair and face dripping wet.

"What happened to you?" my dad asked, trying not to laugh.

"I went to turn on the water in the kitchen sink, but someone put a rubber band around the sprayer button, so the water shot out right into my face."

"Hmmmm," said my dad, turning to look at me, "I wonder who that 'someone' could be?"

"Happy April Fools' Day, Mom! Now, smile for the camera and say cheese," I said as I took a picture of her with her cell phone. "I promised Kasey and Kelly that I would send them a picture."

"So this was all their idea?" said my mom. "I should have known!"

"Was writing on my face their idea, too?" asked Suzie.

"Yep." I nodded.

"Those two are such little tricksters," said my dad.

"I know. They are so crazy. They always have the best ideas!" I said.

"And they're always getting into trouble," said my mom. "That's why we call them Double Trouble!"

"Look on the bright side, Mom. At least you won't have to take a shower this morning," I said, "since you already took one in the kitchen sink."

"Very funny!" said my mom. "Why don't you go downstairs and clean the water up off the floor while I change into some dry clothes."

"Sure thing, Mom!" I said, bounding down the stairs two at a time.

I went into the kitchen and grabbed some dish towels to soak up the huge puddle of water on the floor. *Wow!* I thought to myself as I mopped up the floor. *She really got soaked!*

Just then my dad walked into the kitchen. "Should I be worried, Freddy?" he said, laughing. "Do you have anything planned for me?"

"Not this year, Dad," I said. "Maybe next year."

"You'd better be careful at school today. You never know who might play a trick on you."

I grinned. "You're right, Dad. You never know what might happen!"

CHAPTER 8

April Fools' Day: Part 2

"Nice outfit," Josh said as I got on the bus.

"Same to you," I said, laughing. "Is your underwear on backwards?"

Josh nodded. "Yep. How about you? Did you turn your tighty-whities around?"

"Yes, I did! I have everything on backwards, just like Miss Clark said."

"So do you have it?" Josh whispered to me.

I patted my pocket and smiled. "Yep. I got it right in here."

"Be careful," Josh said. "You don't want to smash it."

"Don't worry. I'm taking really good care of it."

"This is going to be awesome," said Josh.

"I know. I can't wait," I said. "Max is always playing tricks on other people. Now it's finally time for him to be tricked."

"So when it's snack time, are you going to give him the cookie, or do you want me to?" asked Josh.

"I think you'd better do it," I said. "Max scares me."

"He scares you because you let him scare you," said Josh. "You've got to stop being so afraid of him all the time."

"I know, I know," I said. "You're right, but today I still want you to give him the cookie."

Josh laughed. "Okay, no problem. Why don't you give the cookie to me so I can put it in my pocket."

We made sure no one was looking, and then

I quickly passed the cookie to Josh. He hid it in his pocket.

"Max is going to be so surprised," Josh said, laughing.

The bus pulled up to school, and we hopped out.

When we reached the classroom, Josh said, "Oh no! Freddy, look!"

"What?"

"It looks like we have a substitute today." The person standing at the front of the room had black hair. Miss Clark has blond hair.

Chloe, Max, and Jessie walked in. They were all wearing their clothes backwards.

"Look, Jessie," I said. "We have a substitute."

"Good!" said Chloe.

"Good? Why is that good?" asked Jessie.

"Because now Max has to be on his best behavior."

"Says who?" said Max.

"Miss Clark always tells us to be on our best behavior when she's not here," said Chloe. "Now Max can't play any tricks on me."

"It's a bummer Miss Clark isn't here," I said. "She told us that April Fools' Day was one of her favorite holidays. Too bad she's missing it."

"Yes, that is too bad," said the person at the front of the room.

"Wait a minute," said Josh. "That person sounds just like Miss Clark. Doesn't she, Freddy?"

"Yes!" I said. "Exactly like her. Maybe she has a twin sister."

Just then the person turned around. "April Fools'," said Miss Clark as she took off a black wig. "It's really me. I was just wearing this wig."

"That was a good one, Miss Clark," said Josh. "You had us fooled!"

"You sure did," said Jessie.

"See, Chloe?" said Max. "Miss Clark really is here."

Chloe ignored him and went to put her stuff in her cubby.

Max walked over to her.

"Get away from me!" Chloe yelled.

"Fine," said Max. "I just thought you might want to know that you have a spider on your back."

"What?" said Chloe. "A spider?"

"Yes, a big black one," said Max.

"Help! Help!" Chloe screamed as she ran around in circles. "Someone get it off! Someone get the spider off me!"

"Come over here, Chloe," said Miss Clark. "Let me see."

Chloe ran over to her and was jumping around like a monkey, waving her arms and screaming. "Get it off! Get it off!"

"Stop jumping around," said Miss Clark. "I need to look at your back."

Chloe stopped jumping.

"I don't see anything," said Miss Clark.

"It's on my back, and it's big and black. Max said so."

"Oh, Max said so," said Miss Clark. "Really?"

"Yes!" said Chloe. "Get it off! I hate spiders!"

Miss Clark looked at Max. He was laughing hysterically. "Ha, ha, ha, ha, ha, ha!"

"What's so funny?" said Chloe.

"I think you've been tricked," said Miss Clark.

"What?" said Chloe.

"Ha, ha, ha, ha, ha!" Max continued laughing. "April Fools'! There is no spider on your back."

"OOOOOOOO!" Chloe growled. "You are such a big meanie, Max Sellars."

"You were jumping around like a monkey," said Max. "It was so funny."

"Well, I didn't think it was very funny," said Chloe. "You'd better watch it, Max," said Chloe. "You never know when someone might do something to you."

"Yeah. Right," said Max. "No one's going to play any tricks on me."

Josh and I looked at each other and smiled.

After we put our things away, we started on our morning work, but all I could think about was snack time. It seemed like the day was taking forever.

"I made a special treat for you all for snack time today," said Miss Clark.

"Really?" said Jessie. "That was so nice of you!"

"What is it?" asked Josh.

"Brownies," said Miss Clark.

"Brownies," said Max. "I love brownies!"

"Oh, I'm so glad," said Miss Clark, "because I baked them myself. If you all sit down, I will give you each one."

We sat down, she took the cover off the container, and started passing out the brownies.

"Wait! What's this?" said Max, holding up a brown piece of paper in the shape of the letter *E*.

"It's your 'brown *E*,'" said Miss Clark laughing. "Gotcha again!"

"Good one, Miss Clark," said Jessie. "You really are good at April Fools' Day pranks."

"Bummer! I really wanted a brownie," said Max, pouting.

"I don't have a brownie," said Josh, "but I have your favorite cookie. Do you want one?"

"Yes. Say yes," I whispered to myself.

"You have Oreos?" said Max. "I don't have any because I finished the box yesterday. My mom has to go buy some more."

"I'm happy to share one with you," said Josh. "Here you go," and he handed Max the Oreo.

I held my breath.

Max took a big bite.

I waited.

The next thing I knew, chewed up pieces of cookie came flying out of Max's mouth and sprayed all over his desk. "Ewww! Ewww! Ewwww!" he yelled as he coughed and spit some more.

"April Fools' Day, Max," said Josh. "Gotcha!"

Max glared at Josh, and the rest of us laughed so hard we thought we would pee in our pants!

Josh gave me a high five. "Happy April Fools' Day, Freddy!"

"Happy April Fools', Josh!"

Freddy's Fun
Pages

FREDDY'S TOP TEN APRIL FOOLS' DAY PRANKS

To play on your friends and family!

1. Put sugar in the salt shaker, so when someone picks it up to put salt on his eggs, the eggs taste sweet.

2. Put some green food coloring in the bottom of a cereal bowl and cover it with cereal, so when someone pours milk in the bowl, it turns green.

3. Shake a can of soda before you hand it to someone to drink. When she opens it, the soda will explode in her face.

4. Put a gummy worm in someone's sandwich, so when he bites into it, he'll think he's eating a real worm.

5. Put a blown-up balloon in the toilet and close the lid. When someone opens the lid to go to the bathroom, the balloon will float out.

6. Draw on someone's face while he is sleeping (using washable markers, of course!).

7. Take the filling out of an Oreo and replace it with toothpaste. Then put the cookie back together and give it to a friend.

8. When someone asks for a glass of water, squeeze some lemon juice into the glass before giving it to her.

9. Stuff some toilet paper in the toes of someone's shoes, so when she tries to put them on, they don't fit.

10. Poke some small holes in the bottom of a plastic cup, so when someone uses the cup, the drink will drip on his lap.

Remember, pranks shouldn't be *too* mean— be creative, but don't let anyone get hurt (or hurt feelings).

Happy April Fools'!